# Tiny Tortilla

## Arlene Williams

### illustrated by G. Brian Karas

**DUTTON CHILDREN'S BOOKS**  **NEW YORK**

CIP Data is available.

Published in the United States by Dutton Children's Books,
a division of Penguin Young Readers Group
345 Hudson Street, New York, New York 10014
www.penguin.com/youngreaders

Manufactured in China
First Edition
10 9 8 7 6 5 4 3 2 1
ISBN 0-525-47382-3

To Andrew Peyton Hervey—
as you grow, may you become
all that you imagine.
And gracias, Rosalinda, for your
friendship and advice.

A.W.

Dreaming of a hot, tasty tortilla, Juan Carlos pulled one bristly weed and then another from the garden. He stopped and sighed. He had been working hard all morning, but there were so many weeds.

He gazed toward town, thinking of the old woman in the plaza making tortillas at her stand. It was long past noon, and he was so hungry.

So he snuck out of the garden, past the stiff, wiry ocotillo and the little sand dune beneath it, and scurried down the trail. He crossed the dry arroyo, hopping from rock to rock as if the old creek bed held water. He passed the tall saguaro cactus where a gila woodpecker had carved a nest. Then he raced to the plaza.

Juan Carlos pulled a coin from his pocket and handed it to the old tortilla woman.

She shook her head. "All my tortillas are gone. You will have to wait until tomorrow."

"Wait?" Juan Carlos cried. "No! I'm too hungry!"

"I know. It is very hard to wait," the old woman said with a wink. "That's why I keep some special, special masa dough for times like this."

She brought out a glazed clay bowl. In it was the last little bit of masa. "My hands are tired, so it will be up to you to shape the masa into a tortilla," she said.

Juan Carlos looked at the tiny ball of masa. "But," he said slowly, "it is *muy pequeña.*"

"Yes." The woman nodded. "So you must work the masa patiently. If you do, you'll see . . . it will be more tortilla than you ever imagined."

She took the dough and showed him how to pat it flat by passing the masa back and forth between her palms. Her hands fluttered faster and faster as they clapped. *"Palma-palma-palmadita. Palma-palma-palmadita,"* she sang as she gave it a *pat-patta-pat.*

She winked again at Juan Carlos. "Remember . . . be patient. Don't take a bite till it's done."

Juan Carlos nodded. "But how will I know?" he asked.

"When it's so thin . . . and so light . . . take a deep breath and count out three more pats. Then you will see what a tiny tortilla can be."

Juan Carlos left the plaza. He was very hungry,
and he wished he could eat his tortilla. But it didn't look
thin or light. It just looked *muy pequeña*—very little.

Stopping beside the tall saguaro, he sat down to make his
tortilla.

*Pat-patta-pat* went his hands. *"Palma-palma-palmadita.
Palma-palma-palmadita,"* he sang as he worked the tiny tortilla
between his palms.

The sun grew hot on his back. "Señor Sol, go away," he
muttered. He thought of the weeds in the garden and knew
he should hurry back to his chores. He felt hungry, as well—
too hungry to pat his tortilla even one second more.

So he opened his mouth wide but stopped, remembering what the old woman had said. He took a deep breath and counted: *Uno, dos, tres.*

He gave the masa three more pats between the palms of his hands.

Suddenly the tiny tortilla grew bigger and bigger and bigger until it became a floppy, yellow sombrero that settled softly over him.

It felt lovely and cool under the tortilla sombrero, and though he knew he should get back to the garden, he felt so tired from all those *pat-patta-pats.* So he curled up beneath the hat and took a little siesta.

A hot blast of wind woke him as it lifted the sombrero. The tortilla sombrero swirled up and up into the air. Juan Carlos jumped to catch it but only caught the brim. The sombrero ripped and blew away, leaving Juan Carlos with an even smaller ball of masa than when he began.

Juan Carlos frowned at the masa. *"Muy pequeña,"* he grumbled and moved on to the edge of the arroyo to finish making his tortilla. *Pat-patta-pat* went his hands. *"Palma-palma-palmadita. Palma-palma-palmadita,"* he sang as he worked the sun-warmed dough.

The wind whooshed and swooshed, bringing black, billowy clouds into the sky.

Soon it began to rain, and the arroyo filled with swirling water.

"Señora Lluvia, go away," he muttered. He wiped the rain from his forehead, wondering if he would still be able to cross the rocks in the arroyo and get back to the garden. He felt hungry, as well—too hungry to pat his tortilla even one second more. Besides, the dough was surely thinner now. Perhaps the tortilla was done.

He opened his mouth wide, but stopped, remembering what the old woman had said.

So he took a deep breath and counted: *uno, dos, tres.*
He gave the masa three more pats between the palms
of his hands.

Suddenly the tiny tortilla grew bigger and bigger and bigger until it became a small, yellow boat—a *chalupa*.

Juan Carlos stepped into the *chalupa,* and it took off, spinning around and around as it raced down the arroyo.

All at once, the rain stopped, and the churning water disappeared, leaving Juan Carlos in a deep *laguna* whose walls rose high around him.

And, to his dismay, the tortilla boat had sprung a leak and was filling with water.

He climbed out onto a narrow ledge in the wall of the *laguna* and grabbed for his *chalupa*. He could only catch hold of a small piece of the side before the rest of it sank into the pool with a *bubble, bubble, glop.*

Juan Carlos frowned at the masa he was holding. It was even smaller than before. *"Muy pequeña,"* he grumbled and started all over again. *Pat-patta-pat* went his hands. *"Palma-palma-palmadita. Palma-palma-palmadita,"* he sang as he worked the rain-freshened dough.

The wind whooshed and swooshed, blowing his damp hair across his face. He began to shiver.

"Señor Viento, go away," he muttered as he wiped the hair back from his forehead.

He felt trapped on the ledge and alone and hungry—too hungry to pat his tortilla even one second more. Besides, he was certain the dough was very thin now. Perhaps the tortilla was done.

He opened his mouth wide but stopped, remembering what the old woman had said. So he took a deep breath and counted: *uno, dos, tres.*

He gave the masa three more pats between the palms of his hands.

Suddenly the tiny tortilla grew bigger and bigger and bigger until it became a *pluma muy grande,* a huge feather, which caught the wind like a kite and lifted him up into the air, far above the *laguna.*

Juan Carlos held the yellow feather fast against the wind
and steered back toward the garden.

Just then, the woodpecker in the tall saguaro swooped down and snatched his tasty tortilla feather away.

He tumbled into the sand dune, clutching only the very tip of the quill.

With a sigh, he sat up and began to work the wind-dried dough into a tiny ball, no bigger than a kernel of corn. *"Palma-palma-palmadita. Palma-palma-palmadita,"* he sang as he gave the dough a *pat-patta-pat* to make it flat.

Sure enough, it was thin and very light, but it was *muy, muy pequeña.* It was the tiniest tortilla he could ever imagine.
He took a deep breath and counted: *uno, dos, tres.*
He gave the masa three more pats between the palms of his hands.

Suddenly the tiny tortilla grew bigger and
bigger and bigger until it became . . .

the great big tortilla he had dreamed of back in the garden.

He took a bite and grinned. It tasted like *el sol*, the sun—very hot. It tasted like *la lluvia*, the rain—very fresh. It tasted like *el viento*, the wind—so soft and airy.

Savoring the last mouthful of his tortilla, Juan Carlos slipped into the garden and began to pull one bristly weed after another. With each tug, he thought of that tiny ball of masa and remembered how many *pat-patta-pats* it took before the tortilla was flat. *"Palma-palma-palmadita. Palma-palma-palmadita,"* he sang to himself. And before he knew it, the garden was done.